9·4·2₹

VAMPIRE SLUGS ON CALLISTO

VAMPIRE SLUGS ON CALLISTO

JACKIE  FRENCH

Illustrated by
Sarah Baron

Catnip
PUBLISHING LTD

CATNIP BOOKS
Published by Catnip Publishing Ltd
14 Greville Street
London EC1N 8SB

This edition first published 2006
3 5 7 9 10 8 6 4 2

First published in Australia in 2003 by Koala Books,
4 Merchant Street, Mascot, Australia 2020

Text copyright © Jackie French 2003
Illustrations copyright © Sarah Baron 2003

A CIP catalogue record for this book is available
from the British Library

ISBN 978 1 84647 005 9

Printed in Poland

www.catnippublishing.co.uk

To the kids of Bolinda Primary
with many thanks for all their vampire slugs
Lots of love
Jackie

What's worse than mutant cockroaches?

What's worse than your best friend
going on holidays without you?

PART ONE

Vampire Slugs on Callisto

CHAPTER 1

There are lots of nasty things that can happen to you on Earth these days. Trust me, I used to live there.

Mutant cockroaches can ooze into your food dispenser, so when you think you've dialled up a Yummee Yeastee burger all that comes out is a blob of cockroach doo (which looks a bit like a Yummee Yeastee burger). So if you're headed to Earth, take my advice — *sniff* before you bite.

Mutant rats can swim up the sewerage pipe and bite your bum when you're on the toilet. (No, it didn't happen to me, and if it did I'd never say so. Too embarrassing!)

One kid on our corridor was chased around his bedroom all night by a virtual gorilla that had got

loose from a floating hologram advertisement for Footie Snax — well, anyway, that was his excuse for not doing his homework.

But you'll never, *ever* be attacked by vampire slugs on Earth. Because you only find vampire slugs on Callisto, the *nicest* planet in the universe.

Nice, that is, except for *vampire slugs*.

CHAPTER 2

It was a nice day at our café. It's always a nice day on Callisto — well, they used to be until the vampire slugs arrived, but I haven't got to them yet.

The ploddy-plod birds were singing loudly, in between chomping at mangoes and sunflowers and all the other goodies to be found in the gardens and farms or that just grow wild on Callisto.

Dad was in the kitchen, throwing pizza dough into the air to make one of his supanova pineapple pizzas with banana meatballs (I used to think pineapple pizza was the best food in the universe until I discovered banana meatballs). Rosemary, my stepmum, and I were painting the house and the café to get ready for the Harvest Festival.

Dad and I hadn't been on Callisto for the last Harvest Festival. The Harvest Festival is held every year, and we'd arrived here just after it had finished. (Callisto years are two months longer than Earth years, because it takes Callisto two more months to orbit its sun, which means I don't get a birthday as often, which is *totally* bureaucratic. And, anyway, Callisto doesn't have proper months because its moons zap around the planet in just a few days instead of about 30 days like Earth's, but it takes too long to say, 'Hey, guess what happened 31 days ago', so we just say 'months' instead.)

Where was I? Oh, yeah, the Harvest Festival.

The Harvest Festival is BIG on Callisto. I was really looking forward to it. Everyone said there was lots of eating and presents and eating and dancing and eating and wishing everyone happy harvest and eating...

Well, that kind of sums up Callisto.

Everyone *loves* eating on Callisto, not to mention cooking and trying to get everyone to have just one more bite of their caramel custard tarts or pineapple fudge or blueberry pavlova.

That's because years and years ago Callisto was settled by organic gardening lovers. They didn't

like the way really yummy fruit and vegetables were disappearing on Earth to make way for varieties that you could store for ten years in a coolroom, or that bounced instead of splatted if you dropped them, not to mention all the other things (like blue sky) they loved that were disappearing too.

Well, Rosemary and I were slopping away with the paint and Dad was slapping away with the pizza dough and the bees were buzzing and the passionfruit plopping off the vine next door and the air was scented with mangoes and roses and the great smells of everybody else's cooked lunches wafting up Blackberry Pie Street, when suddenly...

*Whooopa whoopa whoopa...*there's this hovercraft up above us.

'Hey,' I said peering up at it. 'It looks like it's going to land here!'

Rosemary grinned and wiped her hands on her overalls. 'Yep,' she said. 'I've got a surprise for you, Sam.'

'A surprise! For me? Yay!' I said. 'We're all going for a picnic in the hovercraft over at Fish and Chips Lake?'

'No,' said Rosemary.

'You and Dad are going to let me have hoverflying lessons?'

'Sorry, kid. Not till you're sixteen,' said Rosemary.

'Um...it's a pet kerfopulus?'

'I didn't know you wanted a pet kerfopulus,' said Rosemary, interested.

Well, I'd never said I did, because a pet kerfopulus costs about a month's barter credits since you can only find kerfopuluses way across the planet. I'd never even seen one, only read about them. But they are supanova soft and floppy, and they've got big brown eyes, and you can ride on them (even though they are only about as high as my waist) because kerfopulus are strong, and I *really* wanted one.

'Well, what's the surprise?' I demanded. I was getting excited now.

Whooopa whoopa whoopa...the hovercraft hovered even lower.

'Well,' said Rosemary, 'you know how you

were saying you miss Cherry since she went to visit her Auntie Biscuit?'

'Yeah,' I said.

'Well, guess what?'

'I'm going to visit her too?' I cried.

'No. I've invited someone to spend the holidays with you!' Rosemary smiled all over her big Callisto-type face.

My grin slipped a bit.

I mean, Rosemary is supanova fantastic as stepmothers go, but she's still an adult, if you know what I mean. And adults just have no idea of who you might want to hang out with.

'Oh,' I said. I tried to pull my grin back from my toes. 'That's...nice. Who is it?'

'It's my nephew!' said Rosemary.

'A boy?'

'Yes,' said Rosemary.

My grin sank past my toes and started burrowing into the ground. 'How old is he?'

'Just your age!' said Rosemary, grinning as though she was giving me the most fabulous present in the solar system.

'I know you're going to be great friends!' she said. 'He's from the fishing fleet — they never come onto land you know — and I thought, well, with you at a loose end soon and the Harvest Festival coming up, this would be a great time for him to visit and see a bit of life on shore!'

She beamed at me.

I tried to find my grin but it had oozed out of

Vampire Slugs on Callisto 17

my toes and started running over to Fish and Chips Lake without me, so I forced a weak smile instead and tried to say, 'Oh, what a supanova idea'. But all that came out was 'Oh'.

Rosemary suddenly realised I wasn't exactly jumping for joy. 'You'll really like him, Sam,' she assured me.

'What's his name?'

'Broccoli,' said Rosemary, just as the hovercraft landed on the road outside the café — except it's not really a road, because it's all grass and flowers instead of bitumen, and there are mushrooms when it rains, but it's where you walk to get from house to house so I suppose it's a road.

And there he was.

CHAPTER 3

He was taller than me and skinnier. (No, I am not fat. Not by Callisto standards anyway. It's just that over the last year on Callisto I've made friends with a lot of supanova triple-decker hamburgers with beetroot, tomato, pineapple, lettuce and pickled carrot slices, and they sort of still stick close.)

He had red hair, a red nose and he looked like a fish. Well, okay, I've never actually seen a fish with red hair, but apart from that he was pure fishface.

And he *smelled!*

'Hi, Auntie Rosemary,' he said, then looked at me the way I was looking at him, and I didn't even stink.

Well, that got me seething like a nuclear reactor in meltdown. What right had he to look at

me like that? I wasn't the one with red hair and fish pong.

'Hello, Broc dear,' said Rosemary, enveloping him in one of her giant hugs (Rosemary is a builder and she's BIG). 'This is Sam. Sam, meet Broc,' and she grinned at us like she thought we'd be the best friends in the universe.

Old Fishface gave me a look like I was a bit of ploddy-plod bird poop, then handed this great parcel to Rosemary. 'I brought you all a present,' he said.

'Thank you, Broc!' said Rosemary, opening it like it was the Golden Sword of Orion. But it wasn't. It was a dead fish.

Well, that explained the fish stink anyway. It was the deadest, pongiest fish I'd ever seen, or smelt. But, after all, it was a present, so I couldn't be too rude. I just said, 'Yuck. You expect us to eat that?'

Fishface smirked. 'It's a wigglefin,' he informed me. 'They're the most delicious fish in the universe and very rare.'

'For which noses throughout the universe are grateful,' I said.

Rosemary laughed. 'Wigglefins don't stink once they're cooked,' she said, grabbing Fishface's

Karrisak. 'Come on in and meet Sam's dad and get settled, Broc.' She gave him another hug. 'It's going to be so good having you stay with us!'

Fishface looked at me and I looked at him. Then we went in to find Dad.

CHAPTER 4

The next day was Monday, except on Callisto Monday is called Mangoday, and I had to go to school.

Correction: WE had to go to school. Me and Fishface.

'Have a good day, you two!' called Rosemary, as she headed out to the workshop. Rosemary was building chairs for the Harvest Festival, though I couldn't work out why we needed so many new chairs. But who knows with adults?

'Enjoy your lunch!' yelled Dad from the kitchen. He was pretty flat out too. He'd decided to invent a new type of fudge for the festival and was trying out all sorts of different flavours.

Dad had packed leftover wigglefin in a bun with lettuce and tomato and some of Mrs

Honeybun's nectarine chutney into our LunchPaks. We'd had the rest of the wigglefin the night before. It had been okay. Well, all right, it had been the most supanova delicious fish I'd ever eaten, but I wasn't going to tell Fishface that.

In fact, Fishface and I hadn't said anything directly to each other yet.

We walked down the road in silence. The only sound was the squish of the odd mushroom under our feet, the thud of ripe mangoes falling off Mr Lamington's trees and Mrs Geranium calling over the fence.

'Yoohoo! Samdolyn, dear!'

'Hi, Mrs Geranium,' I said. 'This is Fishf... I mean, this is Broc. He's my step-cousin.'

'Lovely to meet you, Broc,' beamed Mrs Geranium. 'I just thought you two little honeypots might like to take a few of my apricot jam drops to school! And I made some chocolate and banana cake yesterday and a few asparagus quiches.'

'Why thanks, Mrs Geranium. We'd love them,' I said. Mrs Geranium's kids have all grown up and moved across the planet and she doesn't have anyone to feed, so you have to be kind to her.

'Hey, shark attack!' said Broc, happily gazing at the jam drops. 'Thanks, Mrs Geranium.'

Well, he didn't have to be *that* kind!

Mrs Geranium beamed. 'I'll have some fresh lemonade and mango ice-cream waiting for you when you come past this afternoon,' she promised.

'Shark attack!' said Broc again.

I waited till we were past Mrs Geranium's and had walked down into the cool gully forest of apple, pear and plum trees with wild strawberries growing underneath. It was strangely quiet in the forest today. Normally the ploddy-plod birds are ploddy-plonking away so loudly you can hardly hear the fruit fall off the trees as they peck it, but today all I could hear was the hum of bees, and my footsteps and Broc's.

But I was too angry to bother about the ploddy-plods for long.

'Why did you go and say that to Mrs Geranium?' I demanded. 'Now she'll spend the whole day cooking afternoon tea for us, and Dad'll be miffed because we can't eat our dinner.'

'It's the jam drops!' said Broc. 'We hardly ever see jam drops out at sea.'

'Huh! You just live on fish I suppose,' I said.

Broc regarded me haughtily. 'There's nothing

wrong with fish!' he said. 'And the hovercraft drop other stuff out to us when they pick up the catch. But jam drops — well, they're still a treat.'

I began to see why Rosemary thought it would be a good idea for Fishface to spend some time with us. 'You mean you *never* come to shore?' I demanded.

'Why bother?' said Broc. 'Shore's boring. No waves or whirlypools or lightning leaping from cloud to cloud.'

'Yeah,' I said. 'We're really deprived. We don't even have sharks or giant octopus or...'

'How would *you* know?' said Broc rudely. 'You haven't been on Callisto all that long anyway.'

'Look, Fishface,' I said. 'Some of us don't have fish eggs for brains. We can learn about a place without having been born there.'

'Fish guts!' swore Broc. 'The only thing you cockroaches know is...'

'WHAT did you call me?' I yelled.

'Cockroach!' sneered Broc. 'That's what lives on Earth these days, isn't it? Mutant cockroaches!'

And that's when the school bell rang.

CHAPTER 5

School on Callisto's okay. In some ways it's a zillion times better than Earth — we get to use *books* and *paper* just like we were millionaires or something. But in other ways it's really old-fashioned. Like you get a real teacher standing up in front of you, not a virtual image that some bureaucratic programmer has dreamed up, and you get to know kids from kloms away, not just from your corridor.

Oh, and there's food too.

I suppose teachers everywhere in the multiverse have power over the kids they teach, but on Callisto it means that you have to eat whatever new dish or food combination your teacher's dreamed up over the weekend.

'I've got banana fritters and strawberry pistachio ice-cream for you all to try!' announced Mr Cumquat. 'And as soon as you've finished we'll start on the geometry.'

Someone groaned. 'Please, sir, can't we have the geometry now!'

'After your ice-cream,' said Mr Cumquat

Vampire Slugs on Callisto

sternly. 'Now, I want you all to appreciate how I've got the strawberries mixed smoothly through the cream, and...'

I didn't mind. I like ice-cream. I noticed that Broc was gutsing into it as well. But the rest of the class sort of groaned and ploughed their way through the ice-cream till they could get to the interesting stuff like maths.

It was nearly time to go home when it happened. Mr Cumquat had finished telling us all about quadratic equations and then, like teachers always do, he asked, 'Any questions?'.

I don't know why I did it. I suppose I was in that half-dream state you get into when you're waiting for the bell. But, before I could stop myself, I put up my hand.

'Please, sir, where have all the ploddy-plod birds gone?'

I suppose I'd been brooding on it all day without realising it. And, come to think of it, I hadn't been woken up by ploddy-plod calls this morning either.

Mr Cumquat blinked. 'What?' he asked.

'Where have all the ploddy-plod birds gone? There were zillions around yesterday, but I didn't see or hear even one today.'

Mr Cumquat looked at me kindly. 'Ploddy-plods nest over on Big Banana Island around this time. They'll be back by the Harvest Festival when they've hatched their eggs.'

Someone giggled behind me. Old Fishface Broc. 'I thought you knew everything about Callisto,' he hissed.

I ignored him, but my face was burning red. I wished Cherry was there — nothing ever seems as bad with a best friend beside you. But she wouldn't be back for months and...

'Now for tonight's homework...' said Mr Cumquat.

CHAPTER 6

I stomped back through the fruit forest. Broc trailed behind me.

I wasn't going to talk to him. I wasn't going to look at him. I wouldn't even spit on him if he was on fire and a million mutant cockroaches were waiting to munch his ashes.

Suddenly I stopped. Something was different about the fruit forest, and it wasn't just that the ploddy-plods were gone. I pulled down an apple tree branch and stared at it.

'What is it?' asked Broc, catching up to me.

I didn't answer, firstly because I wasn't speaking to him, but secondly because I didn't know what it was either, and I certainly wasn't going to give him a chance to call me an ignorant Earth cockroach again.

So I just let go of the branch and stalked off again and didn't tell anyone at all about the

millions of tiny black spots all over the leaves.
Well, not till next morning, anyway.

And by then it was too late.

CHAPTER 7

I saw the first vampire as soon as I woke up. It was slugging along the windowsill above my bed.

I sat up and peered at it.

It was tiny, about as long as a pin and just as skinny, and its back was shiny black with a sort of ruff around its neck just like it was wearing a miniature black cloak. Its tummy was white and shiny, and so was its head, except for what looked like two long red fangs.

I giggled, and Dad stuck his head in the door. 'What's so funny, flowerpot?' (Even Dad was starting to talk like a Callistonian now.)

'That,' I pointed.

Dad came over and peered at it. 'Funny little thing,' he said.

'It looks just like a tiny vampire!' I said. 'A teeny-weeny vampire slug!'

'Poor thing. It must be lost,' said Dad. 'Put it outside where it can eat a leaf or something.'

I picked up the vampire slug and placed it gently on my hand. 'Hey, look,' I said. 'It's trying to stick its fangs into me! You dopey slug, I'm not a leaf!' I leant out the window and placed it carefully on one of the leaves of the grapevine that curled around our house. 'There you are, little cutie pie,' I said. 'Have a nice day!'

Someone peered out at me from under the giant macadamia tree. It was Broc. He had a basket of nuts — he must have been picking them for breakfast. 'Who were you talking to?' he demanded.

'Not you,' I retorted. 'I was just talking to...' then I shut up. Imagine if it got around school that I'd been talking to a slug! How embarrassing!

Dad made macadamia nut pancakes for breakfast — triple supanova yum! — then Rosemary dashed out to her workshop to make even more chairs for the Harvest Festival. Dad made another pot of pineapple fudge and started getting the lunch menu ready and polishing the glasses and all the zillion other things you need to do to keep a café running, even one like ours where most customers come just to relax and escape their friends and relatives trying to feed them all the time!

People don't need to buy food on Callisto!

Broc and I set off for school together. I didn't want to walk with him, of course, but I was trying to be polite. I felt sorry for Rosemary having such a droop (a soggy Callistonian fruit that grows in the Southern continent) for a nephew without adding to it by being rude to him.

Well, *really* rude anyway. (Saying things like 'Move your feet, Fishface, or we'll never get there!' doesn't count.)

We'd passed Mrs Geranium's (she had meatballs with peanut sauce and rice crisp nutties and a whole bowl of freshly-picked raspberries for us this morning) and had entered the forest before I noticed.

All the trees had tiny little vampires on them!

The black dots I'd seen yesterday must have been baby slugs, I realised. But they'd grown!

'Hey, look,' I said. I was so fascinated that I forgot it was Fishface I was talking to. 'I saw one of these on my windowsill! And now they're everywhere!'

Broc peered at them. 'They look just like...'

'Tiny vampire slugs!' I finished for him.

'Yeah,' said Broc. He poked his finger at one. 'Hey! It tried to bite me!'

'Ooo, is your finger all mangled and bleeding?' I said. 'That little sweetie couldn't poke its fangs into a lettuce leaf!'

'Yes it could,' said Broc. He pointed. 'See! They're all digging their fangs into the leaves. I bet they're sucking the sap!'

'Well, sap isn't human blood, buster,' I said. 'You know, I saw lots of little black specks on the leaves yesterday! It must have been the baby vampires!'

'They've grown fast then,' said Broc.

'Yeah,' I said. 'It must be all that good Callistonian tree sap. Hey, we'd better keep an eye on the time. We don't want to be late again.'

I glanced at my watch, then realised I didn't have a watch — the chip in my old Earth one had gone kaput, and of course there was no one on Callisto who could repair it.

Watches cost about 50 barter credits on Callisto, which is enough credit to build a new room on your house, or to have 100 dinners — or 'not dinners' really — at our café, or enough to pay for just one leg of a gorgeous, floppy,

expensive kerfopulus. But Dad had said everyone got presents at Harvest Festival, so I was really hoping that I might get another watch then.

'You know,' said Broc slowly, 'if those slugs grew all that much last night, how big do you think they'll be by tomorrow?'

'I bet they don't grow at all,' I said. 'They're probably all grown up now. Don't you have these slugs where you come from?'

Broc looked at me pityingly, so I began to hate him all over again. 'You don't get slugs on fish,' he said.

'Well, we did on Earth,' I lied. 'Great big slugs that crawled off the fish and into your brain at night so that you'd never be able to do a quadratic equation again!'

'Yeah? Is that what happened to your brain?' asked Broc. And then the bell rang, which was really good luck for Broc or I'd have...

Well, I don't know what I'd have done.

Something, anyway.

What's worse than a
small vampire slug?

PART TWO

CHAPTER 8

But I was wrong. The vampire slugs kept on growing. In fact, they doubled in size every day.

By Figday (all right, Friday for you Earthlings) they were as big as my finger. And their fangs looked even longer and sharper and more vampire-like than ever.

I could see Broc looking at them and then looking at me every day as we made our way through the forest. He was just waiting for me to say he was right and I was wrong.

So I didn't say anything. I just ambled on ahead of him, digesting the peanut and banana milkshake and the passionfruit yoghurt pineapple cake that Mrs Geranium had made us in case we starved between our place and school.

School is pretty good on Figdays because we mostly do practical stuff.

Mr Cumquat had made us nutty crisp biscuits and his mum had sent us a basket of her special yellow alpine strawberries, but it hardly took us any time to eat them and then it was time for our 'How to build a hovercraft' lesson.

38

There's only one hovercraft teacher in our whole district. She just goes to a different school every term, so that kids everywhere get a chance to learn how to build a hovercraft. Our school had two hovercraft already, but an extra one was going to be really useful.

Luckily, all that hovercraft building used up the nutty crisps and strawberries — not to mention Mrs Geranium's passionfruit yoghurt pineapple cake — because the School Council had decided that Figday was ice-cream day too, and there were 96 sorts of ice-cream for us at lunch. (Our village, Fullness of Heart, is really proud of its ice-creams, and someone has to eat them and test everyone's new recipes.)

After lunch it was our 'How to breed a tastier passionfruit' lesson, and then we had to feed composted yuck from our school toilets (no, it doesn't pong — well, not much!) into the school plastic-making vats.

Metal is scarce on Callisto, so we make hard plastics for things like hovercraft and solar panel frames out of all sorts of things, like sewage and crab claws. Afterwards, we did a bit of algebra just to have a rest, and then we walked home.

Well, we started to walk home, anyway.

Broc and I shrugged on our SchoolPaks and wandered back down the hill and into the forest.

I was just wondering whether to be nice to him and take him to see Miss Mousse's spotted pigs (if you throw a rockmelon at them they LEAP! right up and grab it out of the air) or take him the other way past the slippery bit at the end of the pig sty and accidentally on purpose nudge him a bit so that he fell in the pig dung. Miss Mousse has a methane digester too — her pig manure makes the gas that Dad uses to cook his supanova meals, which is really weird when you think of it, pig yuck turning into pineapple pizzas with banana meatballs.

But suddenly all thoughts of pigs and slipping step-cousins flew out of my mind.

'Hey!' I yelled. 'What happened to the trees?'

'Great seas and little fishes!' cried Broc. 'What's happened to the vampire slugs?'

'The slugs have doubled in size, that's what,' I said, trying to calculate. 'You know, if they doubled in size every day they'd be really tiny for days, because double of not much is still not much, but when they doubled today while we were at school it made them BIG!'

'Someone,' said Broc airily, 'said they weren't going to grow any more!'

I glared at him. 'Yes-you-were-right-and-I-was-wrong,' I said as fast as I could to get it over with.

'Just look at those trees!' said Broc. He didn't even seem to notice my apology. 'They're as bare as snickerfish bones! The slugs must have eaten just about every leaf in the whole forest.'

I shook my head and pointed. 'No, there's one leaf left. *Oops!*' As we watched, a vampire slug — a giant vampire slug as big as my hand now — stuck its fangs into it.

Slurp! The leaf disappeared. The vampire slug burped, then began to slowly slug its way down the tree.

'The trees look — different — too,' I said slowly. 'Sort of skinny.'

'The slugs must have sucked too much sap out of them,' said Broc grimly.

'The slugs are killing them!' I cried. 'All the lovely trees!'

'And they're still hungry! Look!' Broc nodded at the ground. I looked down. A hundred — no a thousand — vampire slugs were crawling up the hill towards our village.

'They're after the gardens! And the orchards!' I cried. 'We've got to warn people!'

'They'll have noticed already,' said Broc. 'How could anyone not notice slugs vampirising their trees!'

'Especially on Callisto,' I said, staring at the bare branches of the trees. I still couldn't quite believe it! 'Everyone loves their gardens here!'

Broc brightened. 'I wonder how they're going to get rid of them? Hey, shark attack! This is going to be fun! Maybe they'll use a sonic ray like Hildegard did when she fought off the zombie goldfish in...'

'In *Hildegard and the Black Hole!*' I finished for him. I stared at him. Suddenly he looked almost human, and not like a fish at all. 'Hey, do you like the Hildegard books too?'

'They're shark attack!' said Broc. 'I like *Hildegard and the Murdering Mummies of Momda* best. That's where she finds the planet of bones and...'

'No, *Hildegard and the Bug-eyed Monster* is better,' I argued. 'That's where the mud monster...' I stopped. With all this talk about Hildegard we'd nearly forgotten about the dying trees!

'Come on!' I yelled.

We dashed up the track to Fullness of Heart, to see what everyone was doing about the slugs.

CHAPTER 9

It took exactly two seconds to find out what everyone was doing about the slugs.

Nothing.

'Slugs?' Rosemary looked sort of harassed — she was fitting a really difficult bit of carving onto her chairs. 'Oh, yes, the slugs. Look, don't worry about those, they'll be fine. Pass me the tape measure will you?'

'But, Rosemary, all the leaves are gone from the fruit trees and...'

Rosemary sighed. 'Look, kids, I'm really busy. Just believe me, the slugs aren't a problem.'

'But Rosemary...'

'Please, kids, I'm busy! All right?'

'But...'

'Sam!' said Rosemary warningly.

When Rosemary uses that tone you hop it. So we did.

Broc and I walked out of the workshop. I glanced back at Rosemary, busy at her measuring again. 'I don't believe it,' I said slowly. 'How can anyone think the slugs aren't a problem!'

'She's busy with her chairs,' said Broc generously. 'Let's go tell your dad. I bet he'll know what's happening.'

I nodded. 'I bet the customers in the café have talked about nothing else all day!'

We found Dad in the kitchen, cutting up another batch of pineapple fudge. 'Slugs?' he said vaguely. 'Yes, I noticed them at lunchtime. But Rosemary says there's nothing to worry about. Now how about you help me get this fudge into boxes?'

'But, Dad,' I began to argue.

Dad sighed, 'Sam, this is a really busy time of year. I want to do this Harvest Festival properly — it's our first and I want people to think I've made an effort to fit in. So please, just for once, no arguing, and help me with this fudge!'

Fifty-six boxes of fudge on the kitchen table and eighty-three pieces of fudge in my tummy later (Dad makes great fudge), plus afternoon tea (passionfruit jelly with chunks of mango and strawberry in it), Broc and I finally escaped while Dad was stirring his supanova tomato sauce for dinner.

We were having spaghetti and meatballs, and Dad's meatballs are the best in the universe —

Vampire Slugs on Callisto

when you drop one off the table they bounce! This manoeuvre also gets tomato sauce on the ceiling, so I only do it when Dad is in a really good mood. (If you try this at home, make sure that everyone is in a good mood. Oh, and you need to make the sauce from *real* tomatoes, too, all red and juicy, not the hard pink things on Earth.)

Broc and I sat on the front steps and stared at our garden. Or what used to be our garden. Now it was just twigs and slugs.

'Hey, there's Mrs Goodweather.' I waved to her over the road. 'I bet she's doing something about the slugs! Hey, Mrs Goodweather!' I called. I ran down to the fence as she looked up. She had something long and black in her hand.

Was it a slug-destroying laser gun? I wondered. Or a neutron zapper like Hildegard used in *The Bad Baboons of Betelgeuse*?

'Hi, Mrs Goodweather,' I said politely, then, because I was being polite, I added, 'This is my step-cousin, Broc.'

'Hi,' said Broc. 'Is that an atomic bug buster?'

'I haven't heard of that one!' I said.

'Atomic bug busters were in *Hildegard and the Sonic Destroyers*,' said Broc eagerly. 'They...'

Mrs Goodweather laughed. 'Atomic bug buster? No, it's homemade liquorice. It's a special recipe handed down from my great-grandmother. I saw you two little honeyberries on your way to school today and I thought, I know, I'll make them some of my special liquorice.'

'Then it doesn't kill vampire slugs?' I asked.

Mrs Goodweather looked a bit taken aback. 'No,' she said.

'But you're going to do something about the slugs, aren't you?' I insisted.

'No,' said Mrs Goodweather. She looked even more surprised. 'There's no need to do anything about *them*, dears. Now, how about that liquorice?'

'But why not!' I demanded. 'Can't you see all the damage they're doing? They're killing everything!'

Mrs Goodweather shrugged. 'Oh, they'll be taken care of. Don't you worry,' she said vaguely. 'Now, I really must hurry. I promised Rosemary I'd brew up a vat of my homemade polish for her chairs. It's made with my special walnut oil — walnut oil gives wood such a lovely finish, don't you think? There's just so much to do before Harvest Festival!'

Two seconds later we each had a handful of liquorice and she was gone.

CHAPTER 10

I stared at Broc and Broc stared at me.

'*Someone* must be taking the slugs seriously!' I muttered. For the first time I wished Callisto had a police force or a mayor or someone in authority we could go to. But Callisto is too nice to need any of those.

Till now, at any rate.

Broc nodded. 'There has to be someone sensible in this place!'

I tried to think. 'Come on,' I said at last. 'The sooner we find whoever's doing something about the slugs, the sooner we can tell everyone to help them!'

What's worse than being
invaded by vampire slugs?

PART THREE

CHAPTER 11

We went to Damson Featherplucker and Lettuce Juniper's workshop first. Lettuce organises our fire brigade whenever there's a fire in town — well, she keeps the pump in her shed anyway and makes sure that everyone's fire alarm is working.

'Damson and Lettuce make boxes,' I informed Broc as we marched through the gate. 'All sorts of boxes — from giant ones to put your blankets in to tiny boxes for your false teeth.'

Broc stared at me. 'Do you have false teeth?'

'No, of course not,' I said, affronted. 'But if I did have any a box would be really useful.' I peered in the workshop door just as Damson put the final touch on the biggest, sharpest stake I ever saw.

'Hey! Supanova!' I yelled. 'A stake to kill the vampire slugs!'

Damson stared at me. 'No,' she said. 'It's the corner piece for a blanket box. See?' She fitted it into the rest of the framework.

'But look outside! The slugs are eating everything!' I yelled. 'And no one's doing anything at all!'

Vampire Slugs on Callisto

Lettuce shrugged. 'No one has any time to worry about slugs now, Sam. You've no idea how busy everyone is at Harvest Festival time.'

'I'm getting a good idea,' I said sourly.

'Look, don't worry about the slugs. They'll be fine. Just run away and play with your little friend,' said Damson. 'There's a plate of carrot cookies on the table if you'd like a snack,' she added kindly. 'Oh, and take your dad some dried pears — we made too many this year.'

Little friend! Go and play! But I was polite. I didn't say, 'I hope your hair turns into vampire slugs and attacks you in the bath.'

I just stomped out of there without even tasting their carrot cookies or taking a handful of dried pears — which is pretty bad manners on Callisto actually — and Broc stomped after me.

'Now where?' he demanded truculently.

I thought for a minute. 'The Currybushes!' I decided. 'I've never met anyone who loves their garden as much as Mr Currybush! He's got sixty-six different sorts of plums growing and just about every carrot in the universe — red ones and yellow ones and white ones and purple ones.'

Broc shrugged. 'I don't like carrots much,' he said.

'Well, neither do I. But don't tell Mr Currybush that!'

The slugs were in Mr Currybush's garden too, of course — in fact, there wasn't a garden in the whole of our village that wasn't being sucked dry by vampire slugs. But there was no sign of Mr Currybush.

'Maybe he's gone out to buy a laser vampire slug zapper,' said Broc hopefully.

I bit my lip. 'Maybe he's inside sobbing and just can't bear to look at his garden.' I'd never seen Mr Currybush anywhere but in his garden before. 'Come on, we'd better find him!' I lifted my hand to knock on the door, when suddenly I heard a banging round the back. 'That way!' I declared.

We raced around the corner of the house. There was Mr Currybush and his son, Spud. They were hammering at something big and square.

'A vampire slug trap!' I yelled.

Mr Currybush stared at me 'No,' he said, as though I was daft. 'It's a compost bin. We're making them for the Harvest Festival.'

I looked at the compost bins, then I looked at Mr Currybush, then I looked at Spud. I shook my head.

Had the whole village gone mad? Maybe they had, I thought dismally. Maybe the devastation of the slugs was more than they could bear!

And, anyway, why would anyone want compost bins for a Harvest Festival!

'Look, Mr Currybush,' I said gently, in case he really had flipped his lid. 'The slugs have eaten all your garden! They've eaten everyone's garden! And the fruit forest and...and everything!'

'Yes, yes, I know all that,' said Mr Currybush testily. 'Look, why don't you pop into the kitchen and help yourself to some prunes. Take a whole bagful! But we're really busy here. It's the Harvest Festival soon, you know!'

'I'd never have guessed,' I said sourly. 'Thank you, Mr Currybush.'

'Where are you going?' demanded Broc behind me.

'To get a bag of prunes,' I said. 'We're going to really need them! You know what all this means, don't you?'

'What?' demanded Broc.

'No more food!'

CHAPTER 12

We wandered back up the street. It just didn't look like Blackberry Pie Street, Fullness of Heart, anymore. No fruit falling from the trees. No flowers and green leaves. Just twigs and slugs and more slugs everywhere.

I made a face at one, but it didn't seem to notice. It just went on sucking and vampirising away.

'I can't believe it!' I said to Broc. 'Don't people realise? What are we going to eat if the slugs kill everything?'

'Fish,' said Broc. But he didn't sound very cheerful about it.

'They're so involved in getting stuff ready for the Harvest Festival that they can't see what's happening!' I said despairingly.

I really, really wished Cherry was back! Surely

she'd know how to get people to pay attention!

Broc nodded. 'Adults are like that,' he said. 'Remember in *Hildegard and the Villains on Venus* when no one believed Hildegard when she said that the moonmonsters were about to attack and she had to prepare the deadly monster madness potion all by herself?'

We stared at each other.

'A potion!' whispered Broc.

'If Hildegard can do it, so can we!' I said slowly.

Broc nodded. 'All we have to do is work out a potion to get rid of vampire slugs!'

CHAPTER 13

How would you find out what destroys vampire slugs? You would plug your terminal into the galaxynet, or slip on a virtual helmet and swim through the information ocean, or...

That is, you would unless you're on Callisto. Here, you go to the library.

Fullness of Heart's library is full of books! Really and truly, cross my heart and hope the slime virus of Alpha Centauri doesn't rot my toes! They have genuine books, and these aren't even old ones. New books made of real paper, and anyone can go and touch and read them and even borrow them, even if they're not a millionaire.

So we did. But there was nothing in any of them about vampire slugs!

Vampire Slugs on Callisto

'Fish guts!' swore Broc. 'So much for that idea,' he added gloomily, as we wandered back up to our place munching the raspberry slices the librarian had given us. (She'd made us take a dozen eggs to give to Dad too — special ones from her Auracana hens that laid blue eggs and had originally come from South America on Earth.)

'There has to be something that kills vampire slugs!' I said despairingly.

'Of course! Garlic!' yelled Broc. 'Why didn't we think of that before! Vampires just keel right over if they smell garlic!'

'But these are vampire slugs,' I objected.

'All right,' said Broc. 'We'll put in garlic for the vampire bit and something else for slugs. What kills slugs?'

I shook my head. 'I don't know. We don't have slugs on Earth. Yeah, I know I said we did, but we don't. There's nothing for slugs to eat on Earth anymore. All we had was mutant cockroaches and stuff like that. How come you don't know how to kill a slug? You've lived all your life on Callisto! I know, I know,' I added. 'There are no slugs on fish.'

I thought for a minute. 'Salt,' I said. 'Salt will sort of dry them out. Or chalkdust, that'd be better — if I were a slug, I'd hate having chalkdust all over me.'

'We could add some vomit too,' suggested Broc.

'How are we going to get vomit?' I demanded.

'I could put my finger down my throat,' offered Broc.

'Yuck! That's really...' I paused. Actually I was quite impressed by Broc's offer and his obvious commitment to the cause. 'It's so disgusting it might just work,' I told him. 'All right, garlic, chalkdust, vomit, liquorice...'

'Why liquorice?'

'Because I ate too much and the smell of it in my pocket is making me feel sick.'

'Wish we had some old fish guts,' added Broc. He brightened. 'We could dig the wigglefin guts up from the compost heap!'

'*You* can dig the fish guts up from the compost heap,' I told him. '*I'll* do the mixing!'

It was almost time for dinner by now, but what with Rosemary hammering like mad in the workshop and Dad fudging away in the kitchen I guessed dinner was going to be late tonight.

So we made the potion. I was going to tell you how we did it, but trust me, you don't want the details, especially when Broc dug into the compost heap for the old wigglefin guts and tried to pick them up and they went all down his...

No, as I said, you don't want to know.

But the potion looked really great when we'd finished. Well, great if you wanted to kill vampire slugs anyway, which means totally supanova disgusting for anything else. Bits of it were white (the garlic and the chalkdust) and bits were yellow and orange and brown (the vomit) and the liquorice was black and the fish guts were green and putrid purple with flashes of blue that glowed like it had been longing to get out of that old fish so it could show its true colours.

And it smelt. It smelt as bad as the Garbage Planet when it exploded in *Hildegard and the Planet of Putrescence*. It even smelt as bad as the time I left my curried egg sandwich in my SchoolPak all holidays and...

But, no, I'd rather not remember that.

I shook my head. 'If I were a vampire slug this stuff'd make me sick. Even if it didn't zap me, I wouldn't want to vampirise another tree for weeks!'

Broc peered out the shed door. 'It's too dark to put the potion on the slugs now,' he said. 'We'll never see them in the dark.'

'Tomorrow then,' I said. 'At least it's Strawberryday (Saturday) tomorrow. No school!

We can spend the whole day zapping slugs!'
I yawned. It had been a long day, what with school
and slugs and making the potion. I glanced at our
potion in its brightly painted bucket. 'Do you
think it'll be all right here overnight?'

'What's going to eat vampire slug destroyer?'
asked Broc reasonably, just as Dad yelled,
'Dinner!' out the back door.

'Just put the lid on and it'll be fine,' I said.

CHAPTER 14

The slug potion was still there in the morning.

So were the slugs. They were even bigger now, great massive beasties clinging to the bare sad branches, their slimy skins gleaming in the morning light.

I peered cautiously into the bucket. The potion was bubbling gently, except now and then a bigger bubble rose up and went plop!

I held my nose. 'Dis should ged rid of anyding,' I said.

'I hope so,' said Broc fervently. He frowned. 'How are we going to get this stuff on them?'

'Dunno,' I said. 'How about we just splash a bit on the first slug we find and see what happens?'

'What if the slug shrieks in agony and falls off

the tree and squishes us and we die in agony too?' asked Broc practically.

'Um,' I said. 'How about we stand far away and splash it?'

'Good idea,' said Broc.

The nearest vampire slug was up what used to be Mrs Goodsoil's mango tree, but which now looked like a sort of stick model of a tree that some kindergartener had put together.

We approached it slowly, looking for the best angle.

The slug peered down at us, although it didn't take its fangs out of the poor withered mango's branches.

'They've got really beady, nasty eyes, haven't they?' I whispered to Broc.

'Why are you whispering?' he enquired.

'In case the slug hears me.'

'But they can't understand you, so who cares?'

I tried to use my normal voice. But it's hard speaking normally while a giant vampire slug is staring at you. 'Who'll do the splashing? You or me?'

'It's your bucket,' said Broc generously. 'You can be the one who does the splashing.'

'Huh!' I said. 'You're supposed to go all brave and boy-like and say, "No, I'll do it!".'

'I may be a boy,' said Broc. 'But I'm not dumb. Whoever does the splashing is going to get really, really smelly.'

'Oh,' I said. 'Good point.' I thought for a minute, then grinned. I ran back to the house and stuck my hand around the back door — Dad was so busy with his fudge he didn't notice — and grabbed a soup ladle. I ran back and dipped it in the bucket, and scooped out a ladle full of yuck.

I peered at it nervously. What if the slug exploded? What if we'd invented a new yuck bomb? What if the wind changed and I got covered in fish guts, vomit, liquorice and crushed garlic?

But if I didn't throw it the slugs would destroy the world!

So I threw it.

CHAPTER 15

The yuck soared out of the ladle as if it were a low-flying hovercraft. It hit the vampire slug right in the face.

'Bullseye!' I shrieked

'Shark attack!' shouted Broc.

The vampire slug froze, as though nothing like this had ever happened in its life. Slowly, very slowly, it pulled its fangs out of the mango branch.

'It's working!' I cried. 'We've done it! We've done it!'

The slug paused again. It seemed to be sniffing, even though it didn't have a nose. Dark drops of sap oozed from its fangs. Its slimy body began to shiver, and the whole branch shivered too.

'*Hurrah!*' screamed Broc. 'Now all we have to do is make lots more anti-slug yuck and...' he stopped. The slug's front end had risen from the branch. Slowly, slowly it rolled over, till it was

under the branch, clinging with its slimy slug suckers to the wood.

'It's going to fall off any second!' I rejoiced. 'Dead at our feet! Just like the zombie brontosaurus of Betelgeuse fell at Hildegard's feet when...'

Suddenly I stopped too.

The slug was slugging down the tree. *Thloop, thloop, thlooop*...faster...faster. It was like a slug express train now. Down the trunk and onto the ground...

'It's heading straight for us!' shouted Broc. 'Run!'

But I was already running.

We thundered down the garden, then looked back. The slug had stopped. As we looked, it reared up over the bucket and...

Glug, glug, glug.

'It's drinking it!' I hissed. 'That slug is drinking our anti-slug potion!'

'But garlic kills vampires!' cried Broc. 'Not to mention all the other yuck we put in it!'

I sighed. 'I reckon vampires are different on Callisto,' I said gloomily. 'Just like everything else.' I stared back at the slug. It was slurping up the last drops of yuck potion now, and looking wistfully at us in case we had any more.

'I think we'd better go back to the house,' I said cautiously. 'I don't like the way that slug is staring at us.'

So we did.

CHAPTER 16

'Stakes!' said Broc. We were sitting in the café — it was deserted, as everyone was too busy with their festival projects to go out — eating one of Dad's supanova marshmallow raspberry ice-cream pineapple and chopped banana sundaes with a cherry on top.

'I don't want a steak,' I said. 'I'm full of banana and raspberry. But Dad'll cook you one if you like.'

'Not steaks! Stakes!' said Broc impatiently. 'The sort you stab vampires with!'

Light dawned. 'Oh, that sort of stake,' I said.

'Everyone knows that you can kill a vampire by thrusting a stake into its heart,' said Broc.

'But anything dies if you thrust a stake into its heart,' I pointed out reasonably.

'Who cares?' said Broc. 'As long as it gets rid of slugs.' He brightened. 'Maybe if we just stab a few of them, the others will get discouraged and slug away.'

'It's worth a try,' I said dubiously. I wasn't all that eager to stab a vampire, slug or not. 'But it's your turn to do the stabbing.'

Vampire Slugs on Callisto

'Why?' asked Broc.

'Because I sloshed the yuck,' I said.

'Fair enough,' said Broc. He scraped out the last of his sundae. 'Come on. Let's see if Mr Currybush will let us have a stake.'

'Just one? But there are thousands of slugs!'

'Yes,' said Broc reasonably. 'But once we've stabbed one, we can pull it out and use it again.'

To be honest, I didn't feel like stabbing one slug, much less pulling the stake out and doing it again. But anything to save the trees of Callisto!

CHAPTER 17

'Um,' said Broc.

We were standing under one of Mr Currybush's plum trees. He'd just said, 'Yes, yes, anything...' in a distracted sort of way when we asked him for one of his stakes. He didn't even ask us what we were going to do with it.

'What?' I asked Broc.

'Exactly *where* do you think I should stab the slug?'

The slug stared down at us. It was even bigger than the one in the mango tree and even sluggier, if you know what I mean, all oozing and gooey round the edges. Only its fangs gleamed hard and evil.

'Well, where do you stab vampires?'

'In the heart, of course.'

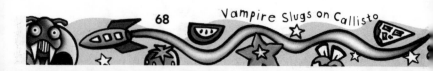

Vampire Slugs on Callisto

'Then stab the slug in the heart, too.'

Broc sighed. 'But where *is* a slug's heart?'

I blinked. I'd never thought of that. 'Why not just stab there?' I pointed to a bulging bit under the slug's neck that looked like it might be sort of heart-like.

'All right,' said Broc doubtfully. He grasped the stake as if he were about to use it to pick peas from his plate and held it up and...

'Not like that!' I yelled. 'Haven't you ever stabbed anyone before?'

'Of course not,' said Broc crossly. 'Who would I have stabbed?'

'Well, I don't know,' I said.

'We don't get passing vampires out at sea,' said Broc. 'I mean, Mum doesn't come in every morning and say, "Wake up, Broc, and by the way, could you stab the vampire that landed on the deck last night, please?". How come you know so much about stabbing anyway?'

'Because I've seen the vids on Earth,' I said patiently. 'You hold the stake like *this*, and then you go like *this!*'

Goooop, the stake landed on the slug's slimy hide.

It went in and in and in...then *ooof!* it suddenly bounced out again.

'Great seas and little fishes,' said Broc. 'Let me do it!'

He grabbed the stake away from me. 'Be my guest,' I said.

Poing! Broc thrust the stake in as far as it would go.

Boing! This time the stake flew out so far it bounced off Mr Currybush's front fence.

The slug peered down at us curiously. It didn't seem annoyed. I wondered if it thought we were playing a tickle-a-slug-today game. Then it gave a slimy sluggish shrug and went back to vampirising the plum tree.

'Fish guts! So much for that idea,' said Broc.

CHAPTER 18

'You know something,' said Broc.

'Mm?' I said. I was beginning to feel a bit depressed.

'I think we're going about this the wrong way,' said Broc.

'Well, of course we are,' I said. 'One slug ate our yuck potion and the other slug thought we were playing tickles.'

'What I mean is...' said Broc patiently, 'we're trying to think up ways that vampire killers destroy vampires. We should stick to what we know best.'

'Well, nothing I know is useful for killing vampire slugs,' I said despondently.

Broc looked smug. 'SupaFishSaks,' he said.

'What are SupaFishSaks?' I demanded.

'Fishing nets — but special,' he said.

'So?' I said.

'I happen to be an expert with SupaFishSaks,' said Broc. 'I should have thought of it before! If we drop a SupaFishSak over a slug it won't be able to move! And that'll stop it sucking at any more trees.'

I thought about it. It seemed pretty foolproof. It even seemed vampire slug-proof. 'Just one problem,' I said.

'What?' demanded Broc.

'We don't have a SupaFishSak.'

'Of course we have a SupaFishSak,' said Broc. 'It's in my Karrisak. I never go anywhere without my SupaFishSak.'

'Why would a SupaFishSak be useful here?' I demanded.

'To catch vampire slugs,' said Broc.

Well, there wasn't any arguing with that. 'Go and get it then,' I said wearily. I was getting a bit sick of trying to destroy vampire slugs, to tell the truth. It was all very well for Hildegard to spend her life battling the mutated mosquitoes of Mars or the roaring throat rippers of Orion. I just wanted to spend my Strawberryday watching the ducks on the dam or catching yabbies or maybe building Callisto's greatest treehouse or even having a go at building a hovercraft from scratch.

But, instead, every tree had been sucked dry by horrible fat slugs and no one seemed to care and I was just about crying, but I didn't, because I never do anything like that. And, anyway, Broc came out with his SupaFishSak just then. So we went off to attack the slugs again.

CHAPTER 19

We chose the smallest slug we could find this time. It wasn't a very small slug — they were all pretty big by now. This one was only about the size of my arm, but much fatter than my arm even after a year eating all the good things on Callisto. It was happily vampirising what had once been an apple tree, but now looked like it just needed to have a rest in one of Mr Currybush's compost bins.

'Right,' said Broc. 'This is the plan. I'll climb up the tree and drop my SupaFishSak on the slug, and you pull the edges from below and tie them up so it can't escape.'

I looked up at the slug. What if it fell on me in shock when the SupaFishSak fell on it? 'How about I climb the tree and you tie up the slug?' I suggested.

'All right,' said Broc. He passed me the net. 'Do you want a hand up?'

'I can manage,' I said a bit shakily. It's not every day you have to climb a tree with a SupaFishSak to ambush a vampire slug. I grasped the first branch

and heaved myself up, then grabbed the next branch and the next.

I looked down. Broc stared up at me. The slug ignored me. 'Now open the SupaFishSak!' yelled Broc.

'How?' I called down. 'I have to use one hand to hang!'

'Then open the sak with the other!' instructed Broc.

'But how...? Oh, I see!' The SupaFishSak unrolled as I held onto the edge of it.

'Now throw!' ordered Broc.

I threw.

It wasn't a perfect throw. It wasn't a perfect landing either. But at least it landed on the slug's back.

'Got it!' I cheered, as Broc gathered the SupaFishSak from below and tied the ends securely. The slug seemed to suddenly realise something was happening. It glanced up at me, then down at Broc. It tried to rear to get a better view, but the SupaFishSak was pulled too tight.

'We've got it,' sighed Broc. 'We've finally found out a way to stop the slugs.'

'As long as we've got another thousand

SupaFishSaks,' I said, gingerly trying to find my footing down the tree.

'No worries,' said Broc. 'We've always got plenty of them. The red weed on the Plenitude Sea makes great SupaFishSaks. All we have to do is...'

'Um, Broc,' I said urgently.

'...call a floater and...what's wrong?'

'I think the slug is moving!' I said nervously.

It was. Unable to go up, it had decided to go down — the tree was shaking as it slugged its way down the trunk. *Thloop, thloop, thloop...*

'Hold tight!' yelled Broc.

'I think I'm going to fall dow...' I began, and then I did, bumping down the branches while I wondered if I was going to find out what a broken leg felt like.

Whumf! I landed on something soft.

'Er, is that you Broc?' I asked nervously.

'No,' said Broc.

I felt underneath me. It didn't feel like Broc either. Not unless Broc had suddenly grown slippery, slimy, slug-like and...

'*Errk!*' I yelled, leaping off the vampire slug. I tried to brush slug slime off my you-know-what.

But at least we had caught the slug. One down, another thousand to go. I peered down at the slug. It didn't seem to mind at all that we'd caught it in a SupaFishSak. It had rolled over so that the rough tied-up bit was now on top — it looked a bit like a bow in its hair, except that vampire slugs

don't have hair — and it was *thloop thloop thlooping* happily over to the next tree.

'Um, Broc,' I said.

'What?' asked Broc. He was staring at the slug too.

'That SupaFishSak doesn't seem to be slowing it down at all!'

'No,' said Broc, watching the slug — SupaFishSak and all — climb the next apple tree.

'It seems to think it's a fashion accessory. Like a new hat or shoes.'

'Fish guts,' swore Broc, watching the slug stick its fangs into the first apple branch. 'All we've done is made it the best-dressed vampire slug in town! Hey, look, there's another slug in that tree already.'

'Maybe they'll fight!' I said hopefully. 'Maybe once there are no fresh trees the slugs will all fight each other and wipe themselves out and...' my voice died away as I watched the two slugs — one dressed in the latest fashion fishing net and the other bare and slimy — happily vampirise their tree together.

I bit my lip. 'Let's go home,' I said despondently.

So we did.

CHAPTER 20

We gave up after that. Hildegard had managed to rid the Planet Zaza of the flesh-eating zombie ants, but there was no way Broc and I could get rid of the vampire slugs.

Callisto was doomed.

I curled up on the big sofa in the living room and Broc sat next to me, not cuddling or anything because that would be really yuck, but it was still nice having someone next to me who understood, and then I started crying.

Me! Crying! But I couldn't help it. The water just leaked out of my eyes and my nose got all runny and then suddenly a big sob started choking me and I just had to let it out.

'Don't cry, Sam,' said Broc. 'Please.'

I looked at him. He looked a bit red about the eyes too. 'I can't help it,' I snivelled. 'I...I just love Callisto, and now it's ruined and we'll have to go live somewhere else and I DON'T WANT TO!'

'You could come and stay with us on the boat,' said Broc hesitantly. 'Your dad could run the café there and we always need ship's carpenters, so there'd be plenty of work for Auntie Rosemary.'

'What's your boat like?' I asked. Somehow I'd never even thought to ask before.

'It's small,' said Broc. 'About the size of your place here. But we're usually linked up with some of the other boats — the school boat or the library boat — that lock in with us most weeks, and then there's the Mullets and the Swiftsails — they've got kids, so they're usually locked in to the school boat too and...'

Well, it sort of took my mind off vampire slugs. Half of me was out there on the Plenitude Sea, leaping from boat to boat or unloading my catch onto the hovercraft. But the rest of me was still miserable and worried and, yes, scared.

That's when Rosemary came in. She looked exhausted as usual and covered in sawdust, and was just staggering off to the shower and plunge

pool when she saw me and Broc and did a double take.

'What's wrong?' she asked.

I looked at her. I'd told her yesterday, but adults never really listen, even when they're as nice as Rosemary. 'It's the vampire slugs,' I sniffed. 'They're ruining everything!'

Broc glared at Rosemary. 'There must be something you can do!' he cried. 'Sam and I have been trying...'

'But nothing works!' I added, just as another sob slipped out while I wasn't watching.

'Oh, darlings,' said Rosemary. She looked like she was trying to suppress a grin. She plonked down between us on the sofa. 'Have you really been worrying about that? I told you it'd be all right!'

'Worry!' I yelled 'We've been trying to save the planet!'

'Just like Hildegard in *Hildegard and the Zombie Ants of Planet Zaza!*' added Broc.

'It's my fault,' said Rosemary guiltily. 'I should have explained properly. But I've just been so busy getting ready for the Harvest Festival, and Sam's dad has been too.'

'Explained what?' I asked.

Rosemary hesitated. 'Look,' she said. 'You'll find out tomorrow in any case.' The grin broke out suddenly. 'And I'd really like to see your faces when it happens,' she added. 'How about you promise not to worry anymore today, and tomorrow...tomorrow I promise you'll realise, well, how Callisto deals with vampire slugs!'

'You've called in an intergalactic pest exterminator and her neutron ship is going to land tomorrow with her super-deadly pest destroyer!' I suggested.

'Nope,' said Rosemary.

'You all bring out your ray guns like Hildegard did!' suggested Broc.

'Nope,' said Rosemary. The grin was even wider now.

'Well, what will happen?' I demanded.

Rosemary stood up and began to brush the sawdust from her overalls. 'You'll find out tomorrow,' she said. 'Now no more worrying? Promise?'

'Okay,' I said a bit doubtfully. I looked at Broc. He gave me a shrug as though to say, what else can we do. Then he nodded.

What's worse than being
attacked by a zombie ant?

PART FOUR

CHAPTER 21

Dad made my favourite pineapple pizza and banana meatballs with tomato and black olive salad for dinner.

I suppose Rosemary must have had a word with him because he was still elbow-deep in fudge for the Harvest Festival. He made stuffed potatoes too, because that was Broc's favourite — Broc said they grew salad stuff like lettuce and parsley hydroponically on their boats, but not potatoes because you really need soil to grow those, and since they were so heavy the hovercraft mostly brought them out rice instead.

Vampire Slugs on Callisto

I forced myself to eat a couple of slices of pizza, well, seven actually, and Broc managed to eat ten stuffed potatoes, but our hearts weren't really in it, and neither were our stomachs.

Would the problem of the vampire slugs really vanish tomorrow? It was hard to believe. But Rosemary seemed so sure...

I managed to eat a bowl of strawberry ice-cream with stewed cherries and a few slices of watermelon and a couple of walnut slices and an apple for dessert, then crept off to bed. Trying to rid a planet of vampire slugs really wears you out. I had just closed my eyes when...

Thloop, thlooop, thloop.

I opened my eyes.

A vampire slug sat on the windowsill, leering at me out of the darkness. Its fat body oozed more slime than ever, and its fangs were stained with leaf and tree sap. It was the biggest, fattest, *meanest*-looking vampire slug I'd ever seen, and by now I'd seen a few. It grinned at me evilly and lifted its fangs and...

Zap! Its fangs went deep into my big toe!

I shrieked and tried to bash it with *Hildegard and the Killer Cockroaches.*

'What's wrong?' Broc raced in wearing his shark pyjamas.

'It's a vampire slug!' I shrieked. 'It's got my toe!' That slug really hurt.

Broc grabbed one end of the slug and tugged.

'*Ow!*' I shrieked. 'Don't do that! Its fangs are in my toe!'

'Fish guts!' swore Broc. He looked round frantically for a weapon. He reached for my hairbrush.

'Are you going to brush it to death!' I demanded.

'I thought the bristles might hurt it enough to make it let go! Hey, I know!' Broc dropped the hairbrush and ran into the bathroom. Two seconds later he was back.

'Soap!' I yelled. 'The slug doesn't need washing! It needs destroying!'

'Just hold on a second!' panted Broc, frantically lathering the soap and slathering it all over my feet.

'Hey, that tickles!' I wasn't sure what was worse — being soaped to death by Broc or being vampirised by a vampire slug! But then suddenly...

'Hey! It's going!' I said. I looked at the vampire slug zapping across my bedroom floor and out the window as fast as its sluggy slime would carry it.

'It's the soap,' said Broc proudly. 'It made your foot taste disgusting.'

'Erk,' I said. I was shaking to tell the truth. Earth vampires might go for your neck but, believe me, being vampirised in the big toe is no joke either!

Dad and Rosemary poked their heads around the door. 'What's up?' asked Dad.

'We heard yelling,' said Rosemary.

'You're too late,' I said. 'A giant slug just tried to vampirise your only daughter. But Broc saved me.'

'It *attacked* you?' Rosemary looked really worried. 'I've heard about the slugs attacking people,' she admitted. 'But that was years ago. I didn't ever really believe it.' She gazed at the slug slithering out my window. 'They are much bigger than usual this year,' she observed.

'Oh, goodie,' I said. 'It's a great year for slugs.' I'd just about stopped shivering now. 'I think I'll sleep with my window shut.'

'Good idea,' said Dad shakily. 'How badly could it have hurt her?' he asked Rosemary.

'I don't know,' said Rosemary. For the first time she really looked worried by the slugs. 'I think we'd better check the whole house before we go to bed. Just in case. This is really unusual, you know.'

'Yeah,' I said. I was feeling a bit miffed, not to mention scared and sore. I'd tried to warn them! I glanced out the window at the mango tree next door — the skeleton of a mango tree with all its sap sucked out. Would I have looked like that in the morning, I wondered, all drained of blood and shrivelled?

'Are you sure the slug problem will be fixed tomorrow?' I asked Rosemary.

'Quite sure,' she reassured me. 'It's as regular as apples ripening! Come on,' she said to Dad. 'Let's make sure the windows are shut and there are no more slugs inside. Sleep well, you two.'

I watched them leave. 'Huh!' I said to Broc. 'I wish I were as sure as she is.'

'Do you need a hand into the bathroom to wash the soap off?' asked Broc.

I shook my head.

My toe felt all right now. It just ached a little like when you get an injection at the doctor's, except this time stuff had been sucked out, not injected in. 'I think I'll keep my soapy feet till tomorrow,' I said. 'Just to make sure they're vampire slug-proof. Hey — maybe the slugs all turn into nice guys overnight!'

It seemed the sort of thing that might happen on Callisto. Broc shook his head. 'I reckon

tomorrow everyone lights their barbecues and has a feast of vampire slug kebabs.'

'Yuck!' I said. 'I'm not eating roast vampire! Anyway, if a stake can't get through slug skin, how would you skewer them and how could your teeth manage to chew them?'

Broc sighed, 'Maybe you're right. Goodnight, Sam. Just shriek if another slug attacks you.'

'Don't worry. I will,' I promised him.

CHAPTER 22

I woke early the next morning. Even while I was asleep I must have been dreaming about the day of doom for the vampire slugs!

What was going to happen? What would I see when I looked out the window?

Dead slugs decomposing all over the place, their guts oozing out across the lawn?

An army of slug hunters sneaking through the undergrowth — well, Mrs Geranium's flower beds anyway — to catch them in the dawn?

Maybe there'd be a terrible slug plague, and they'd start coughing up blood clots and sap clots and all the other stuff they'd eaten?

Maybe...

There was only one way to find out, I told myself. I had to look!

I knelt up in bed and opened the curtains and peered out the window. It was still almost dark.

The sky was grey and pink and orange, and the slugs were...

It was no use. It was too dark to see! Curiosity was burning a hole in my tummy (or maybe I needed breakfast), but I just had to find out what had happened to the slugs first!

Should I wake Broc? I wondered. No. If I snuck out now, I could wake him up later and tell him what had happened to the vampire slugs.

I threw on my overalls and sandals. I wondered for a second if I should put on body armour, then realised there isn't any body armour on Callisto — not even the lightweight armour they use on Earth to stop acid skin burn from atmospheric pollution.

Then I opened the door and crept outside.

The world was silent. Nothing moved. Not even a breeze rustled the dead twigs on the trees.

No *thloop, thlooop, thloop*. No *slurp, slurp, suck*. Not even a single vampire guzzle.

I peered through the dimness. It must have worked! But what was it? What had saved the

world from vampire slugs when even a brave, brilliant kid (me — well, and Broc too, a bit) hadn't managed it?

I tiptoed over to the nearest tree. I was almost there when...

Thloop, thlooop, thloop.

It was coming from Mrs Geranium's place. I froze. Maybe whatever had zapped the slugs had left one?

Thloop, thlooop, thloop.

I froze even solider. That thloop was coming from next door!

Thloop, thlooop, thloop.

And there was more thlooping on our roof — and more coming from Dad's parsley patch and...

I peered through the dimness. The sun was almost rising now, and in the pale pink light I could see...

Vampire slugs! Twice as big as yesterday, which made them HUGE!

And they were all heading in my direction!

Thloop, thlooop, thloop. Thloop, thlooop, thloop.

I was surrounded!

I turned to race back into the house just as this monster vampire slug reared up in front of me!

It was twice as big as the slug last night! It was taller than me and wider and much slimier! Its fangs were as long as Dad's best carving knives and looked twice as sharp. They gleamed in the early morning light.

I took a step back, and then another.

Whump!

I turned.

I'd bumped into the biggest vampire slug of all!

The slime dripped down my arm and onto my overalls. My breath froze in my body. I forced myself to take in air — in out, in out...

Think, Sam, think! I told myself.

What would Hildegard do if she was surrounded by vampire slugs? She'd puff them to powder with her ray gun! I felt in my pockets automatically.

No ray gun.

She'd zap them with her laser rifle!

I didn't even bother checking to see if someone had slipped me a laser rifle overnight.

She...she...

She'd yell for help, I decided, just as my mouth sort of opened of its own accord.

'Hellllp!' I screamed, *'Hellp!!!!!!!'*

Broc's window opened. 'Sam!' he yelled. He took one look at what was happening and clambered out the window. 'Fish guts!' he swore. 'Don't worry! I'll...' His voice broke off as another giant slug reared towards him, its mouth open wide.

'Broc! Get back!' I shrieked. 'Or you'll be slug food too!'

'Sam!' cried Dad. The front door slammed open as he ran out in his pyjamas.

Wham! A vampire slug oozed out from under the porch and lashed him with its tail. Dad went over like a sack of mangoes. The slug began to ooze its way across him. Its slimy bulk hid him from view.

'Dad!' I screamed. 'Rosemary!'

'I'm coming!' yelled Rosemary. She leapt out the door and started banging the slug on top of Dad with her hammer. 'Take that, you brute!' she screamed.

'I'll be all right! Help Sam!' choked Dad.

'I'll...' began Rosemary. Her voice broke off as she swung her hammer at yet another slug bearing down behind her.

Now Broc was swinging something too — the broom, I thought, he's got the broom. Then suddenly I had no time to think at all!

The slug's wet mouth had closed around me. It twisted me from side to side, then dumped me down. Its great damp fangs lunged towards my neck.

Was this the last thing I'd ever see? I thought. A slimy vampire mouth descending over me! Two dirty fangs all covered in sap? 'Goodbye!' I choked, hoping that some of my family would survive to hear my final words. 'I love y...'

What's better than
a dead vampire slug?

PART FIVE

CHAPTER 23

Thodda, thodda, thodda, thodda...

At first I thought it was the beating of my heart. Or was it the vampire slugs' hearts, all excited at eating me and Dad and Broc and Rosemary?

The sound grew louder. *Thodda, thodda, thodda, thodda...*

The slug paused above me. A drip of slime oozed onto my face and began to run across my neck. The slug's great head reared up and looked around.

I wormed away from it. I waited for the great fanged face to look down at me again. But the slug gazed upward, at the sky.

Thodda, thodda, thodda, thodda...

The sound was even louder!

I glanced at Dad. His slug was ignoring him as

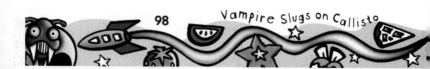

well. Where was Rosemary? Where was Broc? Suddenly their frightened faces met mine, peering round their slugs.

Then suddenly Rosemary began to smile. She pointed upwards.

Thodda, thodda, thodda, thodda...

It was a roar now.

It seemed to take up half the sky.

Then suddenly I saw them! A great dark cloud blotting out the rising sun. Their wings beat like a galaxy of drums. Their sharp beaks shone in the sunlight.

Ploddy-plod birds! I breathed.

The sky was full of ploddy-plods. Then slowly they began to descend, all over the village and the forest beyond. Ploddy-plod birds in their thousands, tens of thousands.

'But...but there are so many!' I cried.

Rosemary's smile had become a grin now. 'They've been breeding! They feed up on the fruit and then they nest on the rocky islands over on the coast — that way the fruit rats can't eat their eggs. Then the baby birds hatch — and by then they're all very, very hungry.'

I peered at the birds. Sure enough, there were big ones, and little ones too, lighter and brighter than their parents. As I looked, one of the parent

ploddy-plods seized a vampire slug in its great tough beak and...

Splurt! The slime spurted across the lawn. *Sploot!* Another slug split in front of it. A dreadful slurping sound was coming from all around — and it wasn't the slurping of vampire slugs either.

The ploddy-plods were having breakfast.

CHAPTER 24

That's when we decided it was a good idea to have breakfast too. Or at least get inside away from slug guts.

We had to climb over the slugs to get to the front door. Some of them were trying to get away — but no slug can *thloop thloop thloop* as fast as a ploddy-plod can fly.

'Burnt biscuits!' exclaimed Rosemary, leaning against the door. 'I thought we were really in trouble then! The slugs have never grown so big before! I reckon all those old stories about slugs attacking people years ago must really be true!' She peered out the window. 'But luckily there seem to be more ploddy-plods this year too.'

'Let's get this straight,' I demanded. 'The vampire slugs eat all the leaves and trees...'

'Then the ploddy-plods eat the slugs!' Rosemary beamed at us. 'The baby ploddy-plods need food to grow big and strong. Ploddy-plods eat fruit the rest of the time — but after nesting or when they are babies they need a really good meal of vampire slug. You see? Everything is fine!'

'It's not fine!' I yelled. 'The garden's full of slug guts and all the trees are bare and the slugs have eaten all the flowers and vegetables and...and...'

Rosemary gazed up at the ceiling. 'Should I tell you?' she said. 'No, I'll let you see for yourself. It'll be much more fun that way.'

'Fun!' I shrieked. Well, I'd had a hard day and it was still only dawn! I'd been attacked by a vampire slug and seen my family about to be slugged too!

'Breakfast time,' said Dad. He looked a bit white around the gills too. 'Who wants waffles?'

'With maple syrup and sliced banana and blueberries and passionfruit yoghurt,' added Rosemary. 'And maybe some mango crush too.'

I gave in. Firstly because my tummy said it wanted waffles and sliced banana with passionfruit yoghurt more than it wanted explanations. And secondly — well, Rosemary had been right about the slugs, hadn't she? So I may as well trust her now.

Sometimes — just sometimes — adults know what they are on about! (But if you tell anyone I said that, I'll spit!)

After breakfast, Broc and I sat on the front steps and watched the ploddy-plods guzzle up the vampire slugs, while Dad went back to his pineapple fudge-making and Rosemary went back to her chair construction.

Those ploddy-plods could really eat. First of all the parent birds would stab a slug with their beaks, and then they and the baby birds would slurp up the oozy slug insides before hopping over to the next one.

Stab! Slurp! Hop!
Stab! Slurp! Hop!

'You'd think they'd burst,' said Broc admiringly, watching a baby ploddy-plod suck up its tenth vampire slug.

'Yeah,' I said. 'I suppose their tummies stretch or something.' I sighed. 'It's funny. I thought I knew everything about Callisto, but now it turns out I hardly know anything at all.'

Broc shrugged. 'Who cares?' he said. 'Anyway, Callisto's a big planet. You should see the Plenitude Sea some time.' He glanced at me a bit shyly. 'You could stay with us next holidays if you wanted,' he added.

'Okay,' I said.

'Really?' Broc gave me one of Rosemary's big grins. 'Shark attack!'

'What's with this "shark attack" business anyway?' I'd been meaning to ask him for ages.

Broc shrugged. 'It's like your "supanova",' he said. 'You know — really good.'

'But sharks aren't good!' I protested. 'Not if they're attacking you anyway.'

'Neither are supernovas,' Broc pointed out.

Well, he had a point. And I was getting a bit bored watching ploddy-plods slurp up the vampires.

So we went back inside to finish off the waffles and help Rosemary polish her chairs.

CHAPTER 25

For three days the ploddy-plods chomped their way through the vampire slugs. The garden was full of slug guts and ploddy-plod droppings, and it stank!

And then it rained.

It rained and it rained, and the trees all sprouted big new leaves and the gardens grew again, and by the end of the month Callisto looked like it always did — but greener and more fruitful than ever, thanks to all the slug and ploddy-plod fertiliser. The ploddy-plods went back to guzzling fruit again. And I suppose a few damp slugs managed to sneak off and lay vampire slug eggs so there'd be vampire slugs for next year's ploddy-plod babies and parents to eat.

And Broc and I and the rest of our class finished building our hovercraft (Mrs Fruitbat, the hovercraft teacher, said it was the best hovercraft any class had ever made!). But the best thing was

that Cherry sent me a cakeogram, which is like an ancient telegram except it's a giant cake, and this one had written on it: 'Having a grate time wish you were here have a grate festivool love Cherry'. Cherry is an even worse speller than me.

And then it was time for the Harvest Festival.

What's better than a
Callisto Harvest Festival?

PART SIX

CHAPTER 26

It was the best Harvest Festival I'd ever been to! Well, all right, it was the only Harvest Festival I'd ever been to, but it was supanova fabuloso!

I was woken up so early it was nearly the night before — I mean it wasn't even eight o'clock yet — by this horrible howling outside my window.

Vampire slugs! I thought. I leapt out of bed, shoved my left foot into my right slipper and got my other foot caught in yesterday's underpants, when suddenly I realised — first of all I was trying to put my underpants on over my pyjamas, and secondly the ploddy-plod birds had eaten all the vampire slugs.

So I shoved my underpants back under the bed and peered out the window.

It wasn't a vampire slug or even a cow with indigestion from too many peaches, plums, pears and mangoes.

It was Dad, and he was singing.

Well, he thought he was singing anyway. Frogs have better singing voices than my dad — though, like he says, frogs can't make chocolate mousse.

And then I realised every other adult in the whole of Fullness of Heart was singing too, only they did it much better than my dad. Rosemary was singing outside Broc's window and there was Mrs Honeycake in her garden and Herb and Saffron from next door and...well, *everyone*.

I dived into the shower for three seconds, quickly dried and put on my best overalls (the ones with ten thousand and one purple bananas embroidered all over them), and then raced up the corridor and — thump! — bumped into Broc.

We grinned at each other.

'Shark attack!' he yelled, just as I shouted 'Supanova!', and then we dived out the front door together.

By now all the adults were out on the road singing or playing musical instruments — old Mr Beetroot had a double bass on wheels and Mr Currybush had a zither and Parsnip Breadmaker had his violin. Dad was clanging two saucepan lids together almost in time with everyone else, which

was a great improvement on his singing, and Rosemary was playing a flute.

As we came out, everyone started on this great long procession down the road, and Broc and I joined in.

Down through Fullness of Heart with its gardens in full flower again and ploddy-plod birds munching in the fruit trees. Through the apple, plum, pear and cherry forest, past the school, which we'd decorated with garlands of flowers and fruit the week before...

All along the way kids poured out of houses and other adults joined us and everyone was singing at the top of their voices:

'Will you come to the land
Of honey and plum trees,
Where bright birds sing...'

Well, if you want to hear the rest of it you'll have to come to Callisto next festival!

Finally, we all came to the village hall, which was decorated with flowers and fruit and great long trestle tables of food and drinks in buckets of ice. Some of the musicians — the ones who could really play, not like Dad — wandered up onto the stage and Broc and I just stared.

'Shark attack!' he whispered.

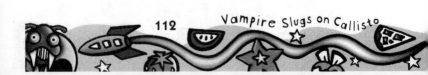

I couldn't say anything. I'd never seen so much stuff in my life!

'What is it all?' I finally whispered to Rosemary.

She grinned. 'Harvest presents!' she said.

'You mean like Dad's pineapple fudge and your chairs and Mr Currybush's compost bins?'

'Well, yes,' she said. 'But the presents we made aren't here.' She laughed. 'We really don't need more chairs and compost bins and boxes at Fullness of Heart, not to mention pineapple fudge! Everything that our village made has gone to the village of Peace and Prosper. All of *these* presents are from the village of Bright Water up in the mountains.'

I nodded.

'That's what happens at harvest time,' Rosemary said, 'one village gives presents to another village, but the villages change every year. Last year we gave our presents to Rejoice and Multiply, and we got ours from Marvellous Mud in the boglands. That's where we got all the bags of dried bilberries and blueberries from and the reed baskets that your dad keeps the fruit and vegetables in. We got all the new glass for the

windows and solar panels from them too — they have good sand deposits and glassworks at Marvellous Mud.'

I frowned. 'But who chooses what goes where?'

'There's a roster,' said Rosemary. 'It's how things get passed around the entire planet — all the things we make get passed to somewhere else and we get stuff from other districts.'

'Wow!' I said, staring at everything piled up all over the hall. 'Who gets what?'

Rosemary laughed. 'You get whatever you want!' she said. 'There's plenty for everyone.' She handed me some bits of paper with my name on them and some bits of string tied in one corner. 'Just tie these on anything that takes your fancy.'

'Anything!'

'Of course! There's lots!'

Broc and I started wandering around the hall. There were great piles of cushions in one corner, all embroidered with ploddy-plod birds and dragonflies, and long lengths of material for clothes or curtains draped over long ladders all up the wall, and a tower of sheets all in bright colours.

'Hey, guess what they do at Bright Water!' I whispered to Broc.

He grinned at me, and suddenly I saw that it was Rosemary's grin. It was weird — I had never really *realised* that he and Rosemary were related, if you know what I mean. 'They must be weavers! I suppose the "bright water" irrigates the cotton and the flax crops for the linen,' he said.

'Yeah!' I left him looking at some rugs and wandered back to the material and stuck my labels on some supanova cloth, all green and yellow stripes — I could just imagine it made into overalls — and Mrs Honeycake cut off enough for two pairs for me. And then I chose some more material in red and purple patches and six pairs of socks (one pair even had a kerfopulus embroidered on them).

Meanwhile, Broc had found a sleepsak — he'd grown out of his old one — and he'd chosen some material too, and then we found the rope ladders sort of hidden behind a pile of fuzzy doormats, so we each grabbed one of those — they were perfect for treehouses.

All around us everyone was laughing and choosing their stuff too, and Rosemary was right — there was more than enough for everyone.

'What happens to all the stuff left over?' I asked Mrs Honeycake.

'It's left in the hall for a while,' she said. 'In case anyone's forgotten something they might need. Then it gets passed on to Sunrise and Happiness, and we'll get the leftovers from Morning Birdsong.' She held a jumper up against me. 'You know, this would look lovely on you, Samdolyn.'

Then it was breakfast time.

All the food had come from Bright Water too, which was great, as I was just a little bit sick of everyone in Fullness of Heart's specialties.

There were watermelons and rockmelons and other fruit I'd never had before that I supposed these other villagers grew with their bright water too — golden ice melons and purple bog cherries and lilyberries and pies with a galaxy of fillings and water ices, which are like sorbets but crunchy and fruity and I ate twenty-seven of them and...

Well, I told you it was supanova!

Then the band played more music and some people sang and Mr Turnip recited this long poem about an explorer who climbed the highest mountain in the universe to pick the berries that grew on top.

And Mrs Daffodil sang another song that I think was rude, but I didn't understand all of it (though Dad and Rosemary were laughing at the bits I didn't understand).

And then the little kids from school played a song on their plukaduks and triangles, and we could almost make out what they were playing. Mr Chestnut brought in his trained hens — they clucked along with him while he sang. Old Miss Parsnip had her troupe of farting geese, and Broc danced this sailor's jig thing, and then he hauled me up on stage to dance with him and then...

What more can I say? You'd have to have been there.

Finally, it was starting to grow dark, and everyone melted away into the twilight. Dad and Rosemary and Broc and I wandered slowly back up through the forest (well, after eating twenty-seven water ices it was pretty hard to do anything fast).

I made it to the front door and collapsed in one of the big chairs (Rosemary had chosen some supanova material to make new covers for them.)

Suddenly there was this loud banging at the door.

'I wonder who that can be!' said Rosemary, in the sort of voice that adults put on when they know perfectly well who it is and are trying to convince themselves that kids are too dopey to know it too.

She opened the door — and there was Dad! I hadn't noticed that he hadn't come in with us.

He didn't look like Dad, of course. He was in this big yellow dressing-gown thing with wheat stuck all over it, and he had a crown of plaited passionfruit vine all decorated with bunches of berries and he was hauling this great chariot full of stuff — well, it was Mrs Beetroot's wheelbarrow but it was painted gold and decorated to look like a chariot.

'It's the Harvest King!' cried Rosemary. And you know what? Dad did look a bit like a king that night too.

So the Harvest King/Dad hauled the chariot/wheelbarrow inside and there were presents for all of us — what Callistonians call 'family

presents' instead of the village presents we'd all got before, because these were things you have to pay for.

There's always masses of food or material or wood or paper on Callisto — things that grow and you just have to harvest. But other things are rarer, and so you have to pay for them — or swap your barter credits anyway. (It's simpler and more complicated than buying stuff on Earth. If you really want to know about it, I'll send you the chapter called 'The Callistonian Credit System' from my social studies book at school.)

So we started unwrapping.

A new chopping knife for Dad — knives cost kilos of barter credits on Callisto because there isn't much metal, and Dad just beamed at Rosemary — she must have had to build someone the biggest deck in Fullness of Heart to get the credits for it.

And Rosemary got a new set of chisels — Dad was really hauling in the credits at the café, and Broc got a pile of Hildegard books as high as the kitchen table and a new series about a guy called Captain Bandicoot, and I got...

'What is it?' I demanded politely, holding it up between my thumb and index finger.

'It's a collar,' grinned Dad.

I looked at it. It was yellow leather with pink and purple beads sewn on it — everyone's clothes and accessories on Callisto are bright.

I tried it around my neck. It was too big. I didn't dare look at myself in the mirror — I could see what it looked like because everyone was grinning.

'It's, um...a really great present,' I said, trying to get some enthusiasm into my voice.

'It comes in two parts,' said Dad gently. Then he opened the door and gave a tug and...

...it was a kerfopulus! The biggest, shaggiest kerfopulus I had ever seen!

'*Plugglif,*' said the kerfopulus, which is kerfopulus speak for 'Hey, am I glad to see you! What's to eat?', which is what kerfopulus mostly say, I've discovered.

I threw my arms around it and gave it a big hug, and the kerfopulus licked my chin, leaving a wet sticky trail across my neck, but I didn't care, I was so happy.

'My very own kerfopulus!' I shrieked, hugging it again. Then I hugged Dad and Rosemary and even Broc before I realised what I was doing, but it was okay because he hugged me back.

Vampire Slugs on Callisto

Then I hugged my kerfopulus again.

'You can ride it to school,' said Rosemary happily.

'Well,' said Dad, beaming at me. 'What do you say?'

There was only one thing to say! I grinned at Dad and Rosemary and Broc, and then at my kerfopulus.

'Shark attack!' I yelled.

Then we all went out into the perfumed night to listen to the ploddy-plods and share leftover pineapple fudge with the neighbours and play with my kerfopulus.

THE CALLISTO SERIES

Jackie French

Hilarious space adventures
liberally flavoured with wonderful food.
Each novel stands alone.

THE CAFE ON CALLISTO

WINNER, AUREALIS AWARDS 2001

What makes everyone burst out laughing
when they discover Sam and her dad are
leaving Earth to set up a cafe on Callisto?

SPACE PIRATES ON CALLISTO

How do you defeat two evil space pirates
and their robotic parrot?
Sam and Cherry find out.